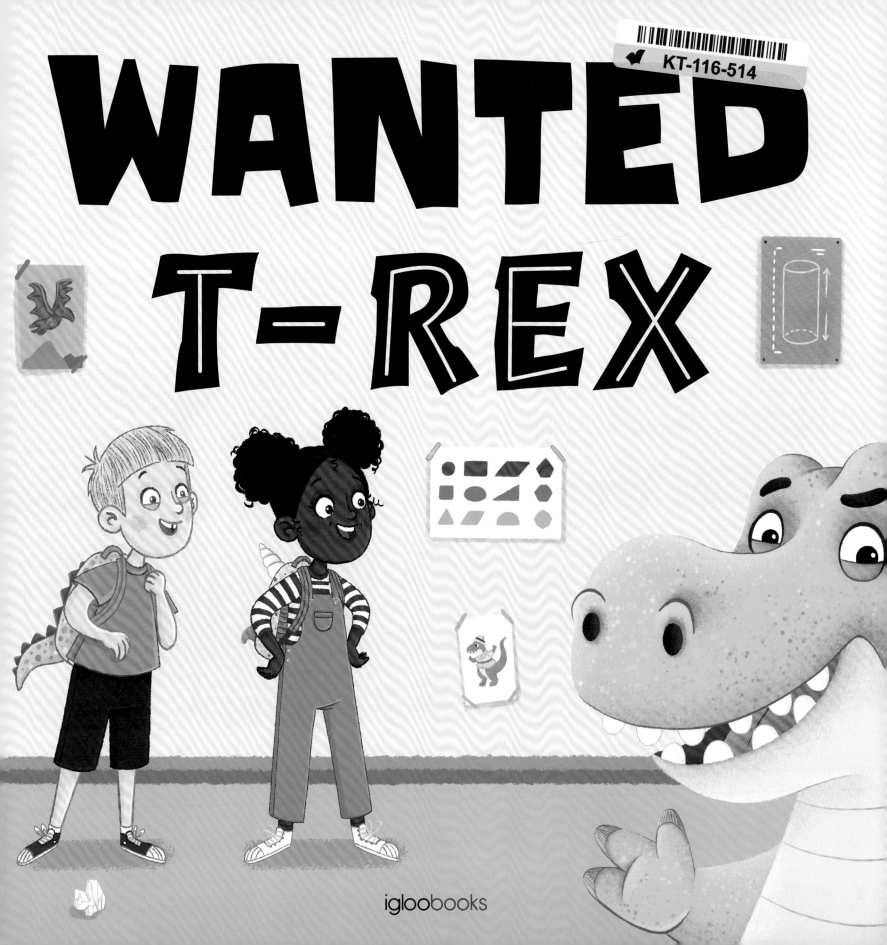

WANTED T-REX

igloobooks

Everybody yawns.
We stare up at the clock.
Seconds seem to crawl by slowly.

TICK...
TICK...

This igloo book belongs to:

....

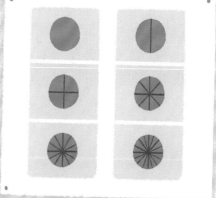

igloobooks

Published in 2021
First published in the UK by Igloo Books Ltd
An imprint of Igloo Books Ltd
Cottage Farm, NN6 0BJ, UK
Owned by Bonnier Books
Sveavägen 56, Stockholm, Sweden
www.igloobooks.com

0221 001
2 4 6 8 10 9 7 5 3 1
ISBN 978-1-80022-647-0

Written by Stephanie Moss
Illustrated by Hannah McCaffery

Designed by Jason Shortland
Edited by Claire Mowat

Printed and manufactured in China

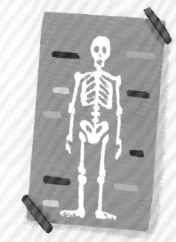

BRRRING!

TOCK!

At last, the school bell rings.
We run and shout HOORAY!
Mr Chalk's dull, boring class
is done for one more day.

We want a brand-new teacher
who will help make learning fun.
We've all had some ideas!
But this is our best one.

TEACHER AUDITIONS THIS WAY

We want someone **BIG** and **TALL** who has a gleaming smile.
They've not been here before (or at least not for a while).

You still haven't got it? Well, their voice would be a **ROAR.**
Oh, okay, we'll tell you. We all want a...

Don't you think a
T-Rex teacher would
be super cool?
We would wake up
early and say,

We can't wait
for school!

Imagine if our dino teacher turned up on the bus!
He'd squeeze himself aboard and would be just like one of us.

"HELLO, CLASS!" he'd shout out,
as he thundered down the hall.
Teachers might be frightened,
but we wouldn't mind at all.

Then lessons would begin. He could take us back in time. No reading from textbooks and no more copying lines.

We'd slide down a volcano,

then go off to explore.

WOO-HOO! We'd all yell.

"Why wasn't school like this before?"

We'd start off with
a science lesson.
Then history, too.

He wouldn't make
it **BORING** like
the other teachers do.

You wouldn't believe if you saw what he did next.
Classes come to life when they are taught by a T-Rex!

Back at school, the other kids would watch with jealous stares.
Dinos love the outdoors. He'd prefer to teach us there.

But PE is much harder, for a T-Rex never tires.
"Can we stop?" we'd call out.
But he just roars, "Higher, higher!"

If a T-Rex was our teacher,
all the bullies would be gone.
And cheaters or gum chewers?
Well, he'd scare off every one.

POP!

Lunch would last for hours
because dinos love to eat.
We'd race out to the playground while
he **MUNCHED** on tasty treats.

He'd never give us homework.
"Yay! Thank you, sir!" we'd shout.
Then instead of marking,
you would find him working out.

If our parents ever met him, they might **TREMBLE** with fright.

But they'd soon get to know him...
... if he promised not to **BITE.**

He'd tell the greatest stories anyone had ever heard.
We'd be so amazed that nobody would say a word.

Yes, if our wish came true, we'd all be the teacher's pet.
A T-Rex is a teacher that we would never forget.